Adapted by Matt Huntley
Based on the teleplay "Pups Save Adventure Bay!" by Jeffrey Duteil
Illustrated by Nate Lovett

A Random House PICTUREBACK® Book
Random House 🏠 New York

© 2024 Spin Master Ltd. PAW PATROL and all related titles, logos, characters; and SPIN MASTER logo are trademarks of Spin Master Ltd. Used under license. Nickelodeon and all related titles and logos are trademarks of Viacom International Inc. Published in the United States by Random House Children's Books, a division of Penguin Random House LLC, 1745 Broadway, New York, NY 10019, and in Canada by Penguin Random House Canada Limited, Toronto. Pictureback, Random House, and the Random House colophon are registered trademarks of Penguin Random House LLC.
rhcbooks.com
ISBN 978-0-593-80840-5 (trade)
Printed in the United States of America
10 9 8 7 6 5 4 3 2 1

Early one day at the Adventure Bay Arena, Skye and Rocky put the finishing touches on a giant loop-de-loop. The racetrack was ready for the Monster Truck Championship!

"Isn't it exciting, Chickaletta?" Mayor Goodway said, watching from the stands. "It's your first monster truck rally!"

Just then, the two best drivers, Boomer and Roxi, drove into the arena in their big trucks.

The announcer, Ron Rapidfire, began to interview the two stars. "Roxi, you've come so close to winning so many times. Is today the day you finally become champion?" he asked.

"I've always dreamed of being a monster truck champion," Roxi replied. "But, win or lose, I just want to put on a show that *rox*!"

"Not me!" said Boomer. "I'm here to win no matter what—even if I have to cheat!"

Everyone was surprised, even Boomer's friend Frank.

"Did I say 'cheat'?" Boomer said. "I meant, um, because I'm so hard to *beat*!"

And with that, the show began!
Boomer and Roxi zoomed along the racetrack, sliding, gliding, jumping, and flipping.

Boomer raced into the big loop-de-loop, then told Frank to push a button. Slippery green oil squirted from their truck.

When Roxi entered the loop, she hit the slimy puddle and slid off the track. Her truck landed hard and flipped over. The front wheels snapped off and rolled toward the announcers!

"Rocky!" Ryder shouted. "See if you can use your forklift to help Roxi."

Rocky raced into action and quickly set Roxi's truck upright.

"Thanks for the lift," Roxi said. "But I've got to stop those tires!"

Roxi popped up on her back wheels and sped after her runaway tires. She stopped them before they could do any damage. The crowds cheered her bravery!

Boomer thought the crowds were cheering for him.

But Mayor Goodway said, "We saw what you did. As mayor, I must disqualify you from this monster truck rally."

"I guess some people don't know a champion when they see one," Boomer mumbled to Frank as they drove away. "Let's find some real fans."

Meanwhile, Roxi was sad because she thought she was out of the competition. "My monster truck's a *gonester* truck. How am I going to be champion now?"

"We can help with that," Ryder said. "Come back to the Lookout and we'll get your truck show-ready in no time!"

Out at Farmer Al and Yumi's Farm, Boomer decided to put on his own monster truck show. He drove through the cornfield and rammed into the silo.

The farm animals scattered as the silo fell over and started rolling away.

Meanwhile, outside the Lookout, Ryder repaired Roxi's truck—and added a few new features. Just then, Farmer Al called and told him about Boomer's monster truck mayhem.

"No rally's too rowdy, no pup is too small," Ryder declared. "Will you help us out, Roxi?"

"This must be my *trucky* day," Roxi said as her Pup Tag lit up.

While Roxi and the rest of the PAW Patrol assembled, the Lookout transformed into the Rescue Wheels' HQ.

"Say hello to the Rescue Wheels!" Ryder announced. The team's new fleet of vehicles appeared on the viewing screen.

"Dude!" Zuma exclaimed. "We're getting monster trucks!"

"And you're going to need them!" Ryder said. He explained that Boomer and his truck were running amuck. They had to help Farmer Al and Farmer Yumi and their animals!

Out at the farm, Skye's truck, which could drive on the ground and also fly, took to the air and rounded up the runaway animals, guiding them to the farm.

"We'd better put their home back where it belongs," Ryder said. Roxi and Rubble worked together to repair the farm and the silo. Farmer Al thanked Ryder and the team for all their help.

"I don't get it, Frank," said Boomer as he drove away from the farm. "I do all the big stunts, and Roxi just does the cleanup— and they cheer for her? I need to find real fans and give them a real show." Then he thought of the perfect location: downtown Adventure Bay! "So much to crash! So much to smash!"

Boomer roared around Adventure Bay's Town Square, determined to continue his one-truck rally. He pulled the statue of Chickalettta over with a chain and tore through Mayor Goodway's tulips!

The mayor quickly called the PAW Patrol, and they raced to the rescue.

"It looks like Boomer has totally taken over Adventure Bay," Ron Rapidfire announced.

"That's right," replied Syd Skedaddle, a reporter. "He's turned every inch of this town into a monster truck stunt track!"

Meanwhile, Boomer's chain had accidentally pulled up a section of train tracks—and a train was coming! It skidded off the rails, rolled through Adventure Bay, and headed toward the Rescue Wheels' HQ!

It soon became clear: Boomer thought jumping over the train while it destroyed the HQ would be his best stunt of the day! The pups had to stop him.

Marshall used his water cannon to make a giant mud puddle, and Boomer slid into it. It was so mucky and sloppy, he couldn't drive out!

Rubble tried to block the speeding train while Chase snagged it from behind with a hook from his winch. But the train kept moving!

Roxi knew she had to help.

Moving a piece of broken track, Skye and Rocky quickly built a ramp. Roxi used it to launch herself over the train and get behind Chase.

Her sticky tires did the trick! Working together, the pups stopped the train before it could hit the HQ.

Roxi's incredible driving skills saved the town, so Mayor Goodway gave her the rally trophy.

"I proclaim Roxi the monster truck champion!" said the mayor.

"Thank you," Roxi said. "But I have to share this trophy with Ryder and the whole Rescue Wheels team. We're all champions!"

Everyone cheered for Roxi and her pup-tacular friends!